Elizabeth: Book Four
WIDE AS WINGS

ANNE LAUREL CARTER

PENGUIN
CANADA

PENGUIN CANADA

Published by the Penguin Group

Penguin Group (Canada), 90 Eglinton Avenue East, Suite 700, Toronto, Ontario, Canada M4P 2Y3
(a division of Pearson Canada Inc.)

Penguin Group (USA) Inc., 375 Hudson Street, New York, New York 10014, U.S.A.
Penguin Books Ltd, 80 Strand, London WC2R 0RL, England
Penguin Ireland, 25 St Stephen's Green, Dublin 2, Ireland (a division of Penguin Books Ltd)
Penguin Group (Australia), 250 Camberwell Road, Camberwell, Victoria 3124, Australia
(a division of Pearson Australia Group Pty Ltd)
Penguin Books India Pvt Ltd, 11 Community Centre, Panchsheel Park, New Delhi – 110 017, India
Penguin Group (NZ), cnr Airborne and Rosedale Roads, Albany, Auckland 1310, New Zealand
(a division of Pearson New Zealand Ltd)
Penguin Books (South Africa) (Pty) Ltd, 24 Sturdee Avenue, Rosebank, Johannesburg 2196,
South Africa

Penguin Books Ltd, Registered Offices: 80 Strand, London WC2R 0RL, England

First published 2006

1 2 3 4 5 6 7 8 9 10   (WEB)

LIBRARY AND ARCHIVES CANADA CATALOGUING IN PUBLICATION

Carter, Anne Laurel, 1953–
Wide as wings / Anne Laurel Carter.

(Our Canadian girl)
"Elizabeth: book four".
ISBN-13: 978-0-14-305447-4
ISBN-10: 0-14-305447-3

1. New Englanders—Nova Scotia—History—16th century—Juvenile fiction. 2. Acadians—
Nova Scotia—History—16th century—Juvenile fiction. I. Title. II. Series.

PS8555.A7727W52 2006   jC813'.54   C2006-900903-1

Visit the Penguin Group (Canada) website at **www.penguin.ca**

Special and corporate bulk purchase rates available; please see **www.penguin.ca/corporatesales**
or call 1-800-399-6858, ext. 477 or 474

For Craig

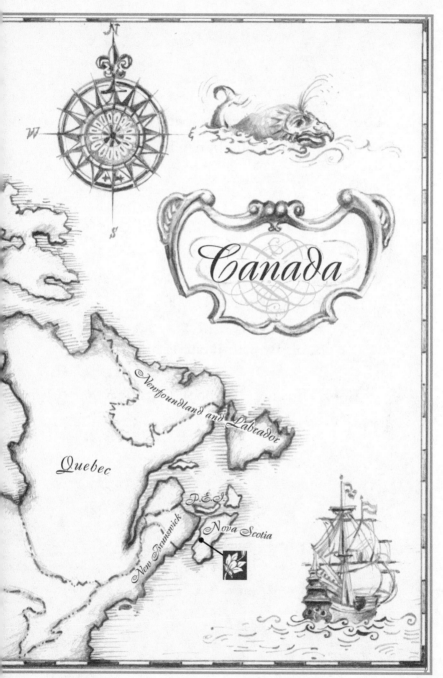

Canada

Newfoundland and Labrador

Quebec

P.E.I.

New Brunswick

Nova Scotia

Marks the location of the story

**Look for the other Elizabeth stories in
Our Canadian Girl**

Book One: Bless This House

Book Two: To Pirate Island

Book Three: A Hornbook Christmas

ELIZABETH'S STORY CONCLUDES

ELIZABETH BRIGHTMAN LOVES HER HOME and friends in Nova Scotia. Recently, she's also discovered she loves to teach. Thanks to her efforts, five-year-old Joshua Porter has learned the alphabet. Even more rewarding has been watching friends her own age learn to read. Mathilde LeBlanc and Ginny, a household slave to the Worth family, surprised everyone with their new skill at the Brightmans' Christmas party. They made such a good impression that Mathilde's parents and older brothers asked if they could attend Elizabeth's school too.

With her mother's help, a home-school should be the perfect way to enjoy the long winter months ahead. There's only one problem. If Mathilde's older brother, Lucien, is going to learn to read at Elizabeth's house every afternoon, then her other friend, Sarah Worth, will have to stay away. Kind-hearted Elizabeth will take that hard. Sarah

Worth, no matter how bossy, has been a good friend. Not only did Sarah save Elizabeth from Pirate Island, but she also found Mathilde a job at the Porters' house.

Unfortunately, Sarah's father, a strict and powerful leader in their community, believes that all Acadians are potential enemies of their English, Protestant colony. Caleb Worth has forbidden Sarah from talking to Lucien LeBlanc, whom she likes, because he is Acadian.

Sarah's interest in boys is not one Elizabeth shares. The only boy Elizabeth can imagine liking is the new baby brother she's praying her mother will give birth to in the spring. Once again their Acadian friends offer their generous assistance; Mathilde's mother will be Mrs. Brightman's midwife.

One day soon England and France will sign a peace treaty, and when they do, Elizabeth is convinced that the LeBlancs will be able to buy a farm and live close by, best friends, forever. But will Caleb Worth let that happen? And what about Ginny and her mother? Will Caleb ever let them buy their freedom, as he once promised? Elizabeth wonders if there is a way she can help all her friends reach their dreams.

CHAPTER N°1

Crunch.

Elizabeth woke to the sound of shovels digging into snow. She ran across her cold bedroom floor to look out her window. It had snowed all night. White drifts were sloped high against the barn, and the LeBlancs were shovelling the wide door clear. Thousands upon thousands of snowflakes continued to drive across the bay toward them.

Elizabeth dressed quickly and ran downstairs. "We can still have school, can't we?"

From the look on Mama's face, she had thousands upon thousands of reasons to say no.

"Please, Mama," Elizabeth begged, not giving her mother a chance to answer. "You promised we could start today. What if it snows from now until spring? Mathilde will never read her French books."

Mama ladled out a steamy serving of porridge. "I've seen many more winters than you, my dear, and the snow will let up. Oh, don't pout like that," she laughed. "We'll start school this afternoon for Mathilde and the LeBlancs. But that snow's too deep for Mr. Porter and Joshua to walk here. The road has no tracks yet."

Elizabeth stirred treacle around in a glum circle in her porridge. Every day since Christmas, she'd asked if they could have school and here it was the third of January. Every day Papa had too much work for everyone. If it wasn't a fence or roof to repair, it was something new to make.

"If you hurry with your breakfast," Papa said from his end of the table, "and help us shovel open the barn, you can feed the animals. Then we can see about a road that needs tracks."

Elizabeth stopped stirring.

"The oxen could use some exercise."

Elizabeth looked up. Papa winked.

"The snow is knee-deep in some places. But our oxen can get through a month of snow."

"Could I take the sleigh to Mr. Porter's and fetch Joshua? Maybe the Worths will let Ginny come this afternoon." Ginny was the domestic slave at her friend Sarah Worth's house. "Please, Papa. It's not far."

"I'd want a boy with you in case you got into trouble. Lucien could take you and Mathilde." There was a warning in Papa's voice. Elizabeth remembered all the trouble she'd caused last fall by getting stranded on Pirate Island. She swallowed her protest. She'd have to let Lucien LeBlanc drive.

The morning dragged by. Finally, when the moment came to leave after the noon meal, Elizabeth stood, clutching the curved end of the sleigh, staring up at Lucien's back on the driver's platform.

"Sit down beside me," Mathilde cried from the seat behind her. "I want to pull the bearskin over us. It's freezing."

"You mean exciting!" Elizabeth couldn't sit. "Go fast!" she begged Lucien.

The sleigh swooshed and slid through the white powder behind the steamy oxen. The road had been travelled by someone that morning, but when the first bump came, Elizabeth tumbled back beside Mathilde.

"And stay there!" Mathilde laughed, tucking the black bearskin over them both. Elizabeth's fingers were numb, and she rubbed them together gratefully under the thick skin. Bear was her least favourite meat to eat but its skin made the warmest blanket.

"Joshua Porter might be at the Worths' house," Mathilde called to Lucien. "We should go there first."

Except for the last snowy days, Mathilde earned money helping Mr. Porter in the afternoons. Joshua's mother had died in childbirth in October.

Everyone, especially Joshua's aunt, Rebecca Worth, doted on the young boy who'd lost his mother.

"Joshua spends every waking minute following Ginny."

"Not Sarah?" Elizabeth asked.

"Not any more. Ever since that week when Sarah was their teacher he has called her *Bossy Sarah.*" Mathilde giggled. "Sarah doesn't like that."

"Joshua Porter is becoming a spoiled brat," Lucien said. "I'd love to have Sarah Worth as my teacher."

Under the bearskin blanket Mathilde nudged her. Elizabeth nudged her back. In spite of Caleb Worth's warnings, Sarah and Lucien continued to flirt with each other. Lucien and his family were French, Catholic Acadians, still considered potential enemies by many Congregationalists. If Lucien were ever caught alone with Sarah, her father had threatened to send him to prison in Halifax.

Elizabeth thought quickly. It wouldn't do to have Lucien wait in the sleigh outside the Worths' house. That would be courting trouble.

"Drop us off at the Worths' house and you go on to the Youngs'. Mama says we ought to ask Maggie and Priscilla to join our school. We'll follow your tracks to the Youngs' house and meet you there."

Lucien nodded. The girls jumped out but the sleigh didn't move on immediately. Lucien stared at the windows of the house as if hoping to catch a glimpse of Sarah. Papa was wrong about his daughter needing Lucien along to keep her out of trouble. It was Lucien who needed them.

She threw a snowball at him. Boys!

"If Caleb Worth catches you here, he'll put an end to our school. Go away, Lucien! Geehaw!" she called to the oxen.

Lucien scowled but thankfully started the oxen moving.

"Caleb Worth!" he called back, louder than he should have. "He's a tyrant!"

Mathilde shook her head as she walked up the narrow, cleared path to the Worths' house. "We shouldn't have let him come with us. He shouldn't be anywhere near Sarah's house."

"He's gone, Mathilde. We'll get Ginny and Joshua and walk over to the Youngs' house. Then we'll circle past the meeting house so we won't come back this way."

Ginny answered the door and invited them into the front hallway. Caleb and Rebecca Worth walked out of his study to greet them. Caleb Worth ignored Mathilde but nodded a welcome at Elizabeth before returning to his study. Luckily for them, he hadn't heard Lucien.

"We're starting school at my house, Mrs. Worth. Can Ginny and Joshua join us today?" Elizabeth asked. Sarah's house had a centre hallway and was twice as grand as any other Planter home was.

"Of course," Sarah's mother said, heading into the back of the house. "I'll find Joshua. He's with Sarah. They'll be right out. Ginny, I expect you to finish the ironing when you get back."

At the mention of Sarah's name, Elizabeth froze. Beside her, Mathilde stiffened too. They hadn't foreseen Joshua being with Sarah.

"What if Sarah wants to come?" Mathilde whispered. "What will we do?"

Ginny whispered back, "You'll have to tell her."

Just as they feared, Sarah appeared with Joshua.

"You're going to have the school at your house? Why don't I come and help?"

Elizabeth, Mathilde, and Ginny eyed one another. No one knew what to say. Elizabeth opened the door and they filed outside.

"Mathilde," Elizabeth said. "You and Ginny best take Joshua over to the Youngs'. I'll be along in a minute."

How could she explain to Sarah without hurting her feelings? She blurted out the truth. "You can't come with us."

A cold wind whipped their skirts around their legs as Elizabeth searched for the right words. "Lucien's driving the sleigh and Lucien's coming to school and your father wouldn't approve."

A look of hope brightened Sarah's face and just as quickly died. She crossed her arms over her stomach as if it hurt.

"You're right," she said dully. "I can't come."

"I'm sorry, Sarah."

"But what's the harm in saying hello?" Sarah's blue eyes were sad. "Papa's so unfair. I'm not allowed to speak to Lucien. Could you give him my regards?" Sarah begged Elizabeth.

Elizabeth shifted uncomfortably and turned her back to the wind. She didn't want Sarah and Lucien to have anything to do with each other. Why couldn't Sarah forget about him? He was just a boy. A teasing, lumbering boy!

"Please, Elizabeth," Sarah pleaded, taking her hands.

Elizabeth remembered all the nice things Sarah had done for her. Finishing her sampler and sewing projects. Getting Mathilde and Papa to save her from Pirate Island. Securing Mathilde the job at the Porters' house.

"All right. But just this once. And then I want you to forget all about him."

Once said, she regretted it. Elizabeth ran to catch up with the others, wondering what trouble would follow her now.

CHAPTER 2

Every precious hour of daylight in January was filled to the brim. Chores in the morning were followed by school in the afternoon. When Elizabeth reached the silver, quiet moment after sunset, she paused to count her blessings. Mama was going to have a baby soon. Madame LeBlanc was a midwife and would make sure nothing bad happened. Best of all, right now, she, Elizabeth Brightman, got to be a teacher every afternoon.

When Mathilde read from her French books, it made no difference that Elizabeth didn't understand. She let her mind go fuzzy and enjoyed the sounds and Mathilde's smile of satisfaction when she finished.

With Papa's help they made French hornbooks for the LeBlancs, and even Joseph LeBlanc joined his wife and sons for the daily lessons. All the LeBlancs made progress but none as quickly as Mathilde.

The hours after supper were busy, with everyone reading or writing by precious candle and lantern light in the Brightmans' parlour.

One evening Elizabeth asked Mathilde to teach her to speak French.

"How do you say 'I am the teacher?'"

Elizabeth repeated Mathilde's translation, but she had trouble with the last word: "*Je suis le professeur.*" Mathilde laughed at the English way her friend said "professor."

As haughtily as possible, Elizabeth said, "I never once laughed at your reading mistakes. A good," she tried the French word carefully again, "*professeur* doesn't laugh at her students."

Mathilde clapped her hands and cried, "*Parfait!* You said it perfectly!"

But Lucien slapped his knee and repeated her original mistake, "*Je suis le* professor," as if Elizabeth's mistake were the funniest thing he'd ever heard.

Every afternoon and evening Elizabeth and Mathilde made a point of choosing a place as far away from Lucien as possible. Little by little Elizabeth's knowledge of French increased. So did the size of Mama's belly. After the LeBlancs had said their goodnights, Elizabeth often sat for a quiet moment by the fire at Mama's feet. Mama let her place her hand on the little mountain of her belly.

"That has to be a boy! He's kicking!"

"Girls kick too," Mama would say with a laugh. "You certainly did."

"Not like that. I've a little brother in there."

At the beginning of February, a merchant vessel dropped anchor in the harbour and Papa took everyone in the sleigh to Fort Edward. Several Mi'kmaq families came from their winter camps to trade, and Elizabeth watched shyly as Mathilde ran to greet the children like long-lost cousins. Mathilde's parents and brothers followed, and Elizabeth felt left out and forgotten until she saw Sarah Worth wave at her.

"I'll be over there with Sarah," she said, leaving her parents to bargain with the sugar merchant.

Sarah ran to meet her, an enormous smile lighting up her face. "Hurry, Elizabeth. There's a merchant with new books," she said, but her eyes were scanning the crowd of people milling about the fort. Who was she looking for? Elizabeth's heart sank. Sarah was looking for Lucien.

"Books?" Elizabeth said, trying to get her attention. "Did you say books?"

Sarah linked arms with her friend, still looking around the fort, and led her to where stacks of books were piled on a wooden bench. "Papa's given me money to choose some."

A short, chubby merchant approached the girls. He pulled on his long, grey beard as he spoke. "What are you girls interested in? I have new chapbooks. Not expensive at all. Only a penny each."

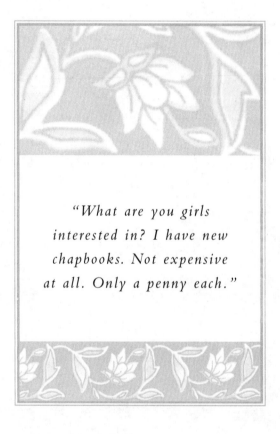

"What are you girls interested in? I have new chapbooks. Not expensive at all. Only a penny each."

Elizabeth forgot about Sarah. Each chapbook fit into the palm of her hand and she picked up one after the other, browsing them hungrily, looking at the title pages and pictures. She didn't have a single penny and she wanted to read all of them.

Sarah gave the merchant four pennies and held out the four books she'd bought for Elizabeth to look at. The first one was a tiny abridged version of *Robinson Crusoe.*

"What do you think? I'll lend them to you when I'm finished. Don't look like that. No, here. Take this one. You can read it first. You can read it in your school."

Elizabeth wanted to refuse but Sarah insisted.

The merchant overheard their conversation. "Do you have a school here?"

"Yes," Elizabeth said proudly.

"Tell your teacher and classmates I'll bring a bigger selection of inexpensive books when I'm back in a month."

Elizabeth imagined him pulling out more of his beard if she told him she was the teacher!

Then someone on the other side of the merchant asked, "Do you have any French books?"

She looked up and wished she were anywhere but here, talking to this merchant. Lucien LeBlanc stood a few feet away eyeing Sarah Worth openly.

What idiots they were! Smiling at each other.

"French?" the merchant spat on the ground. "No one's trading in French any more. Mark my words, we won't see any more French around here, not after they're finished in Paris. What a blessed day that will be."

Lucien edged closer to Sarah, even as he asked, "What's happening in Paris?"

"Don't you know nothing in these backwaters? Why, the kings' ambassadors are meeting in Paris as we speak. They'll be signing a treaty and those French will finally surrender everything to us." The merchant stopped tugging his beard to wave his hand in the air. "North America will be ours. English and Protestant as it should be."

Elizabeth was glad she hadn't bought any books from the merchant. He was a horrid man.

Lucien turned and whispered something to Sarah. Elizabeth looked in the direction she'd last seen Caleb Worth. Sarah's father was still deep in conversation with Captain Mercer. Any minute now he could look up and see Sarah talking to Lucien.

Elizabeth stood in front of her friend, hoping to hide her. With her elbow she rammed Sarah in the back. Sarah kept right on talking to Lucien.

What was the matter with them? Elizabeth looked in the direction of the LeBlancs. They were still chatting with their Mi'kmaq friends.

She elbowed Sarah again. Sarah and Lucien kept right on talking.

Then she caught sight of Mama and Papa beside the sleigh. Mama was leaning against it while Papa loaded bags of supplies inside.

"Papa!" she called anxiously. He turned and stared in her direction. She waved. He said something to Mama and walked quickly toward her.

She didn't have to say anything. Papa had noticed trouble brewing.

"Lucien!" Papa said, stepping between Lucien and Sarah to separate them. Elizabeth turned so that they made a little circle. At least Sarah and Lucien couldn't be accused of talking alone. "And Sarah Worth! Your father will be looking for you, don't you think?" There was a reprimand in Papa's voice, but he continued in a friendly manner. "Where did you get the new book, Elizabeth?"

"From Sarah. She's kindly lending it to me."

"I trust it's nothing scandalous," he said, looking pointedly at the book vendor. "Some of those books are foolish stories."

"Dear me, no!" the merchant answered quickly. "I'd lose my clientele if I sold rubbish, now wouldn't I? Only the best moral literature, I assure you, sir!"

Any moment now Caleb Worth might look over and catch Lucien and Sarah together. Papa seemed to share Elizabeth's worry.

"That's what these girls need. Moral literature. Lucien, can I trouble you? I need help loading the sleigh with supplies."

A long look passed between Lucien and Sarah. Lucien had no choice but to follow Papa.

Elizabeth turned angrily to Sarah. "What's the matter with you?"

Sarah didn't answer. She was staring after Lucien, her face as happy as Elizabeth had ever seen it. Elizabeth grabbed Sarah's arm and yanked her away.

Thankfully, there were no more fearful moments. Papa kept Lucien at his side and Elizabeth kept Sarah at hers. By noon they'd visited all the merchants and it was time to go home.

In the sleigh the Brightmans and the LeBlancs sat with their feet on sacks of new provisions. Everyone talked about whom they'd seen and the news they'd heard. The news on everyone's mind was the Treaty of Paris and the future of Nova Scotia.

"Maybe they'll let the Acadians return," Mama said hopefully.

"Maybe they'll let you buy land again in Nova Scotia," Papa added. "I could help you find land close by. There are still a few good lots left, Joseph."

"The money I've earned at the Porters will help buy it!" Mathilde added eagerly.

Joseph LeBlanc stood silent beside Papa on the platform. The reins were in Papa's hands. Everyone waited to hear what Monsieur LeBlanc would say.

"*Merci*, Samuel. Your family been good to us. But we the only Acadians here. There is no Catholic church, no place for one French family here."

In the distance Elizabeth saw the Congregationalist meeting house and the Planters' homes around it. It was the beginning of a small town. An English, Protestant town. She turned to Mathilde.

"More Acadians will come if you stay. I'll learn French. We'll live side by side and be neighbours."

Mathilde's black button eyes were hopeful. "We'll have our own farm."

"Let's write a letter to Paris this afternoon. We'll ask them to invite all the Acadians back to Nova Scotia."

CHAPTER *N°* 3

Even Mama couldn't believe how quickly
Mathilde took to reading. Mathilde mastered
every reading exercise they could give her in
English and then used the French hornbook Papa
and Elizabeth had made to read her French
books, the treasures Elizabeth had found buried
on Pirate Island.

Mathilde began with the book called *Contes
des fées*. "They're fairy tales," she explained to
Elizabeth. "But that's not why I love them. They're
written by a woman!"

Elizabeth gasped. She bent closely to stare at Mathilde's book. It was bound in shiny, ivory-coloured vellum. There was a single plain decoration on the cover, an impression made in the lambskin by a stamp.

"See!" Mathilde said, turning to the title page. "It says *par Madame d'Aulnoy*. The author was a married lady."

"A woman writer! Did you ever hear of such a thing?"

Mathilde shook her head.

"What will Caleb Worth say if he finds out you're not studying psalms and bible stories but books written by women? He won't let Ginny and Joshua come to our school any more."

Mathilde nodded her head solemnly. "We won't tell anyone about the writer."

"What are her stories about?"

Mathilde looked through the book. It took her a long time to answer. "Most of them start with 'Once upon a time there was a king' and 'a king with a beautiful daughter.' Here's one. It's called . . . just a minute. I have to translate. It's called *The Blue Bird*. See the picture?"

They studied the tiny picture. A beautiful girl stood at an open window in a tower. The drawing was black and white but a few details were painted in with watercolours. Her dress was pink, the bird was an airy blue, and the sun a summery yellow. The girl seemed to be talking to the bird, whose tail was longer than its body.

"I wish I could read it," Elizabeth said longingly.

"I'll read it several times until I can tell it to you in English."

Mathilde's long, black hair swung around the book. It would take her a long time to read the story. She had to sound out the words slowly and guess at many of them.

Mama was helping Maggie, Priscilla, and Joshua, so Elizabeth decided to sit with Ginny, who was working on Table Seven in the Royal Primer.

"Can you read this out slowly while I check each word?" Ginny asked.

Elizabeth did while Ginny pointed to the words:

Truth may be blamed
But can't be shamed . . .
(Were things done twice
All would be wise.
He that would thrive
Must rise by five.
He that is thriven
May lie till seven.)
Help me good hands,
For I have no Lands.
To give to the poor,
Is to add to your store.
Words are but sand,
But 'tis gold that buys land.
Pay what you owe
And what you're worth you'll know.

Ginny said nothing, but her hand was shaking by the last line.

"What's wrong?" Elizabeth asked.

There were tears in Ginny's eyes. "Read the last four lines again slowly," she said.

Ginny sounded them out as Elizabeth read.

Ginny looked over her shoulder before whispering, "See? It says exactly what Mama and I figured. Master Worth's *words* . . . ," she pointed to the words with her fescue. "He promised we'd get our freedom long before he die, after we settled here in Nova Scotia. But Mama and I been thinking things bound to work out more like what it say here. His promise be a heap of sand. We need a heap of gold to get our freedom and we worth every penny of it."

Elizabeth looked at the words and then back at Ginny's face.

"How much gold?"

"We earn a penny here and a penny there. Not enough to buy our freedom."

Elizabeth clenched both her hands. If the Treaty of Paris let the Acadians come back to Nova Scotia, Mathilde's family needed gold to buy a farm. And, here, Ginny needed gold to buy freedom. If Elizabeth had found gold on Pirate Island, instead of books, Ginny and Mathilde could buy their dreams.

"I'll ask Papa to talk to him," Elizabeth said. "But Caleb Worth doesn't listen to anybody."

"He do. He listen to one person outside o' God," Ginny said. "Mistress Rebecca. When push come to shove, she got the strong hand in that house."

Elizabeth recalled what had happened after Ellen Porter, Mrs. Worth's sister, had died last fall. Rebecca Worth had blamed Caleb Worth for not allowing Mathilde's mother to help with a safe delivery. Caleb Worth had slept on the lumpy sofa in the parlour for a long time.

Could Rebecca Worth be persuaded to help Ginny and her mother buy their freedom? She would ask Papa that night at the supper table. The LeBlancs had trapped rabbits, and Mama was making one of Papa's favourite meals: rabbit and dumplings.

"How do slaves buy their freedom?" Elizabeth asked, getting right to the point.

Papa's hand stopped halfway to his mouth. Gravy dribbled off the fork onto the plate below. He frowned and put down his fork.

"I've never owned a slave, Elizabeth. But from what I hear they must go with their master before a notary or a witness and draw up a legal document."

He picked up his fork again and was about to resume eating when Elizabeth asked her next question.

"How much do you think Ginny and her mother would need to buy their freedom from Caleb Worth?"

The fork clattered as it hit the plate. "So that's what this is about," Papa said. He looked at her sternly. "Elizabeth, how many times have I told you not to interfere in adult matters?"

"I'm not interfering. I don't understand slavery. Is it right to own another person, Papa?"

Papa exploded. "It doesn't matter what I think. It matters what Caleb Worth thinks. Others before you have tried to change the minds of slave owners, and others have failed. I'm not prepared to interfere. And you're under strict orders to stay out of their affairs."

He picked up his fork and shoved his food into his mouth.

Elizabeth picked at her food, unable to eat. She'd have to obey Papa. But it didn't mean she'd forget about Ginny's dream or Mathilde's. Somehow she'd find a way to help them both.

CHAPTER N° 4

February was cold and the snow stayed deep so that sleighs and cutters moved smoothly over the roads. Mama said it was a godsend. In the summer the roads were very bumpy and Mama was so large and uncomfortable with the baby, she wouldn't have been able to travel anywhere. On Sundays they bundled up under the bear rug and set off for the meeting house. Elizabeth's woollen stockings itched worse than ever, but it was too cold not to wear them.

Most evenings the LeBlanc family joined them around the fire in the parlour. Sometimes they told stories. Sometimes there were long silences broken only by the hiss and crackle of burning logs. Mathilde was mostly quiet, avidly reading one of her treasures. Elizabeth read and reread Sarah Worth's borrowed chapbooks, waiting for Mathilde to look up and finally retell a story from her French books. A man named Perrault had written the book that was covered in gold-embossed, dark leather. The endpapers were multicoloured and made Elizabeth think of peacock feathers. So far everyone had most enjoyed a story about a girl called *Cendrillon* whose father married a conceited woman who had two daughters. Cendrillon's stepsisters turned out to be even meaner than their mother was.

But one night Mathilde slammed shut the book written by Madame d'Aulnoy. "How can people be so wicked? Why, she's even worse than Cendrillon's stepmother," she cried. Her eyes were fierce.

"Who?" Elizabeth asked. "Who's wicked?"

"Someone in a story," Elizabeth's mother said kindly. "It's just a story, dear."

"Can you tell it? Oh, please tell it."

Mathilde's eyes shone as she told of a girl named Florine who was so beautiful she was known as the eighth wonder of the world. She too had a jealous stepmother who hated her and favoured her own daughter. When Prince Charming visited the court, Florine was allowed to wear only old, soiled clothes. Florine hid in shame, but the prince saw her and fell in love with her instead of the queen's daughter. The queen imprisoned Florine and condemned the prince to become a bluebird for the next seven years. The prince heard Florine grieving at her window because she'd been told he was going to marry the stepsister. For the next two years he visited every night and eventually regained his proper shape.

"Then with a magic spell the stepsister was turned into a sow," Mathilde ended the story. Her eyes were dramatically wide.

"A big one, I hope," Lucien said with a laugh.

A lively discussion followed.

"Could the prince and princess really have understood each other's hearts without knowing each other?" Mathilde's mother asked.

"Of course. That's true love," Lucien argued hotly.

"No," said his papa, reaching for his wife's hand. "It take a long time to know someone. Love grow bigger over time."

Elizabeth stared at Lucien. Were Lucien and Sarah in love? Was Caleb Worth like the evil stepmother keeping them apart? Did Lucien understand Sarah better than anyone else? Was Sarah's real nature sweet and gentle? Or was it a show for him?

Love was impossible to understand. But Caleb Worth wasn't. If Caleb Worth ever caught them together, he'd turn Lucien into something far worse than a bluebird or a fat sow. No magic spell would ever set him free from an English prison.

CHAPTER No 5

Toward the end of March the merchant vessel returned. Elizabeth was more excited than usual to see what the merchants had brought to trade or sell at the fort.

"Last time the merchant said he'd bring more books," Elizabeth said to Papa as they bundled up. "I told him we had a school. He has books that are only a penny each, and Sarah bought four last time, and please, Papa, could I buy *one* this time?"

Their feet made crunching noises in the snow as they walked to the waiting sleigh, with Papa holding Mama's arm as she walked slowly.

Papa winked at her. "Not two or three?"

"*Please*, Papa. It's so lovely to get a new book and I've read each of Sarah's a half-dozen times and Mathilde has told me all the stories from her books twice. I don't mind hearing stories over and over, but I shouldn't always be a borrower but a lender too, don't you think?"

Mama and Papa smiled at each other before they settled in their usual places in the sleigh with the waiting LeBlancs. Mathilde sat on one side of Elizabeth and Mama on the other. Mama quietly slipped something into her daughter's hand. "Pick out two books that everybody might enjoy reading," she said.

Not one, but two! Thrilled, Elizabeth clutched the pennies tightly in her fist, not wanting to show off to Mathilde what she knew her friend wouldn't dare spend. Two pennies. She could give one to Mathilde and still have a penny for a book. But if she gave one to Mathilde . . . she should give one to Ginny . . . and then she'd have none for a book.

"Thank you, Mama," she whispered back and stretched up to kiss Mama's cold cheek. "Am I only to spend it on books?"

Her mother smiled wistfully. "I wish it were twenty more. We do need a library for our school."

Elizabeth's mind went over the titles she vaguely recalled from the merchant's last visit. There'd been books about knights fighting dragons but she doubted Maggie and Priscilla or Ginny would enjoy them. If only Madame d'Aulnoy's book were translated into English. Everyone liked fairy tales.

Once again the tiny fort was bustling with families and soldiers moving among the merchants. The Mi'kmaq had come from their winter camp and were busy trading furs and fish. Mathilde and her family joined them while Mama dragged Papa to look at bolts of soft cotton for baby clothes. Elizabeth spotted the chubby book merchant with the long grey beard and headed quickly for the piles of books.

"Ah, it's the little Miss with the school. I made sure to bring chapbooks to please your readers and your parents. Nothing too risqué, oh no! How about this one here? *The Life and Death of Saint George?*"

Elizabeth groaned inwardly but politely took the proffered book. She wished the merchant wouldn't say so much and would let her look quietly. The first picture portrayed a monstrous dragon and she closed the book and slipped it under the closest pile.

She quickly tried to pick up another but not quickly enough. The merchant pressed an alternative on her. "Not fond of saints and swords? How about this one? It's my last copy. Can't keep it in stock, it sells so well. Let's see now, where's me specs?" He settled small reading glasses on his nose. "That's better. It's a longish title so don't hold your breath. Here it is. *A Narrative of the Sufferings and Surprising Deliverance of William and Elizabeth Fleming Who Were Taken Captive . . .*"

He stopped to stare dramatically at Elizabeth over his glasses. "A frightening tale." He nodded in the direction of the Mi'kmaq. "A story of two children kidnapped by Indians—"

"No!" Elizabeth shouted, waving her hands. She didn't want a story that made her *more* frightened of Mathilde's friends. "No, thank you," she added, regaining her composure. "Please, sir. Could I just look at the books myself? I'll be very careful."

He removed his glasses and huffed. "Suit yourself."

Lost in the piles of books, Elizabeth looked at every title carefully. It was hard to choose, but she found herself drawn to two ghost stories, remembering the night she went to the graveyard with Mathilde and Sarah on All Saints' Eve.

She showed the books to the merchant. "These, sir," she said, giving him her two pennies.

Mama and Papa stood with the LeBlancs and Captain Mercer. She ran over, eager to show Mama her books, but by the intense look on their faces, Elizabeth knew Captain Mercer had important news.

"The Treaty of Paris is very clear," he said. "Yes. The Acadians are allowed to come back."

Elizabeth nudged Mathilde, who nudged her back, laughing.

"We'll buy a farm and be neighbours!" Mathilde cried.

"You can stay!"

But Captain Mercer kept talking, not seeming to share their excitement. "You must remember this is an English, Protestant settlement now. There are more Planters arriving this spring. The land is almost bought up."

Captain Mercer was speaking to Papa but his gaze shifted constantly to Mathilde's parents and older brothers. Only Lucien was missing.

Monsieur LeBlanc spoke quietly to Papa. Elizabeth moved in closer to listen. "Our Mi'kmaq friends have said there are several Acadian families already living around St. Mary's Bay."

"Yes. I've heard of it. Several days south, I believe."

Suddenly Captain Mercer turned his head sharply. Some shouting behind them caught his attention. To Elizabeth's shock, he strode away.

The next seconds were confusing. Elizabeth turned to see what all the commotion was about. To her horror she saw the scene she'd feared most— yet in her excitement to buy books had forgotten.

Caleb Worth stood between Sarah and Lucien. Sarah's face was blotchy with tears while her father shouted and poked Lucien in the chest with the butt end of his whip. Lucien stared at Caleb Worth with outright disdain and loathing.

In the next second all of them ran to help, but Captain Mercer got there first. He put his hand between Caleb Worth's whip and Lucien's chest.

"Lock him up, Captain!" Caleb shouted now at Captain Mercer. "I warned him several times not to speak to my daughter and here he is, flaunting my orders. He's a threat to our safety, Henry. Lock him up before I flog the life off his back."

Captain Mercer motioned to two soldiers and said something quietly to Caleb Worth. Before anybody knew what was happening, the soldiers had Lucien gripped firmly between them and were dragging him away.

"Take him to the cell and lock him up," Captain Mercer commanded.

The proud, angry look on Lucien's face changed the instant he saw them. With the two older LeBlanc boys, Papa had grabbed Joseph LeBlanc to restrain him. He looked like a bull about to charge Caleb Worth. Mathilde and her mother had their arms wrapped around each other and were sobbing.

Elizabeth looked at Mama. Her face was lined with fear.

They watched helplessly as Lucien was dragged to a barrack's cell and thrown in. Then the door was locked.

Sarah's face was blotchy with tears while her father shouted and poked Lucien in the chest with the butt end of his whip.

Elizabeth clutched her two new books against her chest, unable to breathe. In a few short seconds, happiness had left their world. Remorse filled half her heart and anger the other. Anger at herself and at Sarah Worth. Why had she forgotten how Lucien and Sarah had met the last time? Why had she thought only of herself and her books?

Tears streamed down her face. She knew from her feet to her wet cheeks that Caleb Worth had just destroyed all their dreams. No magic charm was going to undo this. He was a horrible, horrible, wicked man.

The next days were painful. Elizabeth had no interest in reading her new books. They sat on the mantel unopened. She didn't want to have school, but Mama insisted they continue. Ginny and Joshua and Mathilde were their only students. Maggie and Priscilla weren't allowed to come because the Youngs were worried about them being with Acadians. The incident had caused a flurry of arguments in the settlement. At Meeting on Sunday no one had approached the Worths, and they arrived and left without looking at anyone, surrounded by a wall of silence.

Mama tried to reassure everyone when school began that afternoon. "We're all worried about Lucien, and we need something to keep ourselves occupied. Papa's doing his best to help. He's gone to the fort to speak on Lucien's behalf, but Captain Mercer says it's partly for Lucien's own safety he's keeping the boy locked up and away from Caleb Worth."

"Caleb Worth will only be satisfied when all the Acadians are in prison. He has Lucien right where he wants to put all of us," Mathilde said bitterly.

Madame LeBlanc's voice was sad. "My boy in prison. God don't hear my prayers."

Mama put her arm around her. "We're all praying for Lucien. He'll be safe. We were all there at the fort. Everybody saw what happened. It was harmless. You'll see. Lucien will be released soon."

Madame LeBlanc shook her head. A deep sadness had taken over her. "We can't live dis way no more. We need a priest and a church and our Acadian family so we be safe."

Elizabeth stared at Mathilde, but Mathilde wouldn't look at her. Her eyes were filled with tears, which she wiped away furiously so they wouldn't fall on the pages of her book.

Only Ginny looked at her. She motioned for Elizabeth to follow her. She picked up the empty bucket from beside the hearth.

"I'll fetch some water," she said, though no one was paying attention.

Elizabeth joined her outside and they walked to the well.

"Things be bad at the Worth house," Ginny said softly. "Master Worth done flogged Sarah."

Elizabeth gasped. Ginny's mouth was tight.

"I ain't never seen Mistress Sarah stand up to her papa like that. She done stuck to her story. She an' Lucien done nothin' wrong. They was talking at the fort like everybody else. After Master Worth whupped her, her mama done took her side. An' now ain't nobody talking to Master Worth an' he sleepin' on the sofa again like da time after Ellen Porter died."

Ginny shook her head. "It sure be a hornet's nest at the Worths' right now. Nobody come visit. They come home after Meeting yellin'. Miss Sarah beggin' you to talk to her next Meeting."

Elizabeth kicked at the hard snow. She picked up the loosened bits and packed them into an icy snowball. The anger she felt toward Sarah was a hard snowball lodged in her heart. She'd been glad when Sarah and her parents had walked out of Meeting to their fancy cutter without staying to socialize.

"I don't want to see her. It's her fault Lucien is in prison." She turned to go inside.

Ginny moved quickly to block her way. "Guess I be mistaken 'bout a lot o' things. Here I thought you was Sarah Worth's *friend*."

"You weren't there that day. You didn't have to watch Lucien get dragged off by soldiers while his family cried. Sarah is bossy and spoiled and thinks only of herself."

Ginny's face showed no expression whatsoever. "Miss Sarah be better than that. An' you all got nice papas. Ain't nothing like Sarah's."

Elizabeth suddenly felt ashamed of herself and how she'd spoken against Sarah. She dropped the snowball.

"Tell her I'll talk to her at Meeting. But no messages to Lucien."

CHAPTER N.º 7

None of the Brightmans made it to the next Meeting. Late in the night, Elizabeth was woken by the slam of the front door. Outside she heard the crunch of boots on snow. It was very dark. She jumped from her bed and ran downstairs. Her mother leaned against the kitchen table, both hands cradling the bulge of her belly. Mama's face scrunched up tight for a few seconds, then relaxed.

Mama smiled at her wearily and held out her hand. Elizabeth took it and asked, "Is it the baby coming?"

Mama smoothed back her daughter's hair and kissed her forehead. "Papa's gone to get Mireille. The contractions started before you went to bed, but I didn't want to worry you. They're very close together now. Help me walk around the house."

Mama leaned on Elizabeth's shoulder, but they no sooner got to the front hall than she stopped, with a sharp intake of breath. Again her face stayed scrunched up tight and Elizabeth waited anxiously until Mama relaxed again.

The front door opened and Mathilde and her mother walked in behind Papa.

"How far apart are they?" Mathilde's mother asked.

"Close now. Every few minutes."

"That's good," Mireille said, nodding, taking over. "Mathilde want to be wit' you. You girls put a big kettle of water on an' I take care of Mama and baby, okay?"

Elizabeth hugged Mathilde. She was so glad to see both of them.

"You look half-asleep!" she whispered.

"You look like you saw a ghost!" Mathilde whispered back. "It's a baby coming. I told you my mama never lost a baby or a mother yet."

They set the kettle to boil while Papa paced the kitchen, waiting for Mireille to tell him what to do. He checked the kettle twice. Elizabeth had watched the births of cows and pigs in the barn, but this was different. This was Mama.

Mathilde's mother whispered something to him, and he came and put his arm around Elizabeth's shoulder. "The house is chilly. Mireille wants you girls to keep a good fire going in the parlour," Papa said. "Maybe you could read in there and when the baby's here, I'll call you."

Elizabeth looked at her mother's face. There was another contraction and her face was tight with pain. She hated to see it. Couldn't Mathilde's mother do something to stop the pain?

Reluctantly, Elizabeth let Mathilde pull her into the parlour. "It might take a long time and your mama doesn't need to see you fretting about her. Looking at your face right now would scare any baby from coming out into the world. Let's read something."

Elizabeth watched in a trance as Mathilde put more logs on the fire and pulled the bearskin rug up close to it. From the mantle Mathilde took Elizabeth's new chapbooks.

"Let's lie on the rug and I'll read."

Elizabeth stopped listening to the sounds in the kitchen and tried to pay attention to the story. Mathilde stumbled over a new word, and Elizabeth explained that an *apparition* was another word for a ghost.

Next thing Elizabeth knew, someone was shaking her awake. It was morning. Light shone through the parlour windows. Mathilde's mother smiled at her. What was Mathilde's mother doing here? What was she doing in the parlour? Beside her on the bear rug, Mathilde lay curled up where she, too, had fallen asleep.

Then Elizabeth remembered. "Did the baby come?"

"*Oui*. Yes, a big baby."

"Is Mama—"

Mireille pointed upstairs. "Fine. Fine. You go see, den I want her to sleep. I clean up. Not'ing like a baby to make a mess."

Elizabeth shook Mathilde awake. Her friend's black eyes opened slowly. She yawned sleepily, looked around, and sat up quickly as if she, too, had just remembered.

"I'm a sister. Come on, we can go see the baby."

They ran up the stairs two at a time, Elizabeth in front. Her parents' door was open and she ran to the side of the bed. Her mother was propped up by pillows, a baby in her arms. Papa moved to the other side to make room for his daughter.

Elizabeth threw her arms around her mother's neck and kissed her over and over. "I was so worried."

"I know, dear. Everything's fine."

Then Elizabeth stared at the baby in her mother's arms. It was tiny. It had a red face topped by a fringe of black hair and two small eyes that were closed tightly. It looked helpless.

"I forgot what a new baby looks like. It's amazing. Is it a boy or a girl?"

"You have a brother. We named him Joseph, after Mathilde's father."

Elizabeth turned around to smile at Mathilde, who was beaming and clapping her hands. "That's a wonderful name."

"Can I hold him?"

Mama nodded.

"Make sure his head is well supported at your elbow. He can't hold his head up yet. That's right."

Elizabeth carefully cradled her brother in her arms. He weighed so little! He yawned and she laughed at the sight of his tiny mouth opening so wide.

"He's saying hello," Papa joked.

Joseph didn't open his eyes. "Hello, Joseph. I'm so glad you're here." He wriggled restlessly, but she rocked him and walked around the room, and he kept right on sleeping contentedly in her arms.

"He's so beautiful." She kissed his forehead, smelling his skin. "He smells good, too! Can Mathilde hold him?" she asked, looking hopefully at her mother.

Mama nodded, and Elizabeth gave him to Mathilde. "Joseph, I'd like you to meet a special person. You can call her cousin Mathilde."

Carefully, Mathilde took the baby and crooned something in French. The room was very quiet except for the creaking of the floorboards as Mathilde walked around the room. Then she eased Joseph back into the waiting arms of Elizabeth's mother.

Papa drew the curtains over the window, dimming the light in the room.

"Time for new mothers and babies to go to sleep. Fathers and sisters and cousins need to get something to eat after all their hard work last night."

Elizabeth's feet hardly touched the stairs as she followed Papa to the kitchen. Monsieur LeBlanc sat at the table and gave his congratulations, and then asked to speak privately with Papa.

Elizabeth hugged Mathilde's mother. "*Merci*," she said fiercely and said a silent prayer. *Thank you for sending the LeBlancs here and keeping Mama and the baby safe. And if You could, please bring Lucien home for them. And don't forget Ginny and her mother. They need to be free. I hope it's not too much to ask.*

Elizabeth took her breakfast into the parlour and ate quickly, not tasting anything. In the kitchen Papa spoke with Monsieur and Madame LeBlanc, but Elizabeth didn't hear a word. All she could think about was the wonder of holding Joseph, a tiny, perfect human being, and how he'd weighed almost nothing in her arms.

CHAPTER N.º 8

On the first Sunday in April, there was still snow on the ground. Papa got the sleigh hitched to the oxen and they took Joseph to Meeting. Mama let Elizabeth hold her brother snugly beside her under the bearskin rug.

All the women wanted to see the new baby after the service. They crowded around Mama and Papa. Elizabeth remembered her promise to Ginny. She found Sarah outside standing by the graves of her aunt and stillborn cousin. There was a sad, pinched look about Sarah's mouth and eyes, as if she'd spent the last weeks crying, but when she saw Elizabeth, she forced a bright smile.

"At least one thing has gone right! I'm so glad you have a brother," she said.

Sarah's kind, selfless words melted the last bit of ice in Elizabeth's heart. She reached for Sarah's hands.

"And I'm sorry about what's happened to Lucien. Papa spoke to Captain Mercer. He's keeping him in prison to keep him safe from . . . ," she paused awkwardly, "from your papa. Until some kind of agreement has been reached."

Tears filled Sarah's eyes and the haunted look was back. "It's all my fault. I should never have spoken to Lucien. I'm so unhappy."

Elizabeth remembered the story about the bluebird. It wasn't fair or right that two people couldn't speak to each other. But Lucien couldn't turn into a bluebird and escape. That only happened in a fairy tale.

"Last week, Papa said he'd force Captain Mercer to deport Lucien. If he does, all the LeBlancs will go with him." Sarah's voice broke. "Mathilde will leave. Everything she said about us will be true. I've refused to speak to Papa or Mama since that day. Mama's caught in the middle. I don't know what else to do. Your brother's birth was timely. It's made everybody, especially my mother, think better of the LeBlancs. If only Mathilde's mother could have helped my aunt." She looked at the graves again. "Joshua's mother would be alive today."

Sarah squeezed Elizabeth's hands as she poured out her worries.

"Elizabeth!"

It was Papa. Everyone was in the sleigh, waiting for her.

"I have to go."

Sarah held her hands a moment longer. "If you see him, please tell him I'm sorry."

Elizabeth squirmed. At least Sarah hadn't asked her to take a letter. She nodded. "There's something you must do in return. Ginny and her mother want their freedom."

A hopeless look passed over Sarah's face.

"That's up to Papa, too. Everything is up to him. I'll speak to Mama about it, but I doubt if he'll give them their freedom. He paid a lot of money for Ginny's mama, and they count on them to make our house run smoothly. But of course I'll try, Elizabeth."

Elizabeth ran to the cutter and snuggled close to Mama and Joseph under the bearskin. As they pulled near their house, Elizabeth heard voices and a commotion in front of the little Acadian house.

Mathilde and her family were arguing, piling packs outside, going in and out of the house.

Papa said, "I thought you were leaving tomorrow."

"Leaving?" Elizabeth cried out, but no one paid attention.

Monsieur LeBlanc looked at the sky. "Snow melt every day now. We go today."

"Load up the sleigh then. I'll take you now."

Mama went to speak quietly with Mireille, while Elizabeth watched Mathilde and her older brothers load things around her.

"Go where? Where are you going?" Elizabeth said, this time taking hold of Mathilde's arm.

Mathilde stared at her. "Didn't you know?"

Papa stood above them, the reins in his hands. He looked uncomfortable. "I meant to tell you this afternoon, Elizabeth. The LeBlancs are going to scout out the St. Mary's Bay area. Their Mi'kmaq friends are taking them. They'll be back in a few days, so don't get upset. They're not leaving for good."

"Scout it out? For what?" Elizabeth repeated dully. The sight of the LeBlancs removing things from their house gave her a bad feeling.

"To see if it will be a suitable place to make a home. Do you want to ride in the sleigh with Mathilde?"

Elizabeth nodded, speechless. When had they planned this? Mathilde climbed in the sleigh, saying nothing, her family with her.

"Geehaw!" Dad called to the oxen.

The sleigh jerked into motion and Elizabeth stared, silent and fearful, at the shoreline. How could this be happening? The LeBlancs' home was *here*. In the distance she saw what she hadn't seen this morning. The icy banks were melting. A new season was beginning. With a week of spring sunshine, the snow would melt completely. The egret might come back any day. In the summer she and Mathilde could go out to Pirate Island in a boat. There was so much to look forward to . . . *with Mathilde.*

Big tears poured down Elizabeth's cheeks and before she could stop herself, she was sobbing.

An arm crept around her shoulder. Mathilde leaned into her. She was crying too.

"Why is this happening?" Elizabeth said between sobs. "I don't want you to go. How can you look for a home somewhere else?"

"I don't want to go either but we have to," Mathilde cried back.

"No, you don't. Who says you have to?"

Mathilde's mother interrupted, her voice gentle but firm. "It be our only hope. It da only way God give us to save Lucien."

Elizabeth shook her head. It made no sense at all.

Mathilde sniffed and wiped her eyes. "Caleb Worth is pressuring Captain Mercer to send Lucien to Halifax on the next ship. If he goes, we go with him. Unless we do something quickly. My papa and yours think if we like the area around St. Mary's Bay, it will be far enough away so Captain Mercer and Caleb Worth will let Lucien come with us."

It was a better solution than deporting the LeBlancs, but even so, Elizabeth couldn't bear thinking about it. Why would God let the LeBlancs go away when they were so close to making this their home again? This wasn't what she'd prayed for.

The Mi'kmaq camp was only a mile up the bay. In misery Elizabeth felt the oxen slow. And then stop. She heard voices calling in a language she didn't understand. Several Mi'kmaq gathered around the sleigh to help unload the LeBlancs' packs.

Mathilde hugged Elizabeth goodbye.

"We'll be back in a few days," Mathilde said, starting to cry again. "Papa promised."

For the first time Elizabeth noticed the misery on her friend's face and in her voice. "I'll keep a journal," Elizabeth said, and she tried to smile. "I'll write down everything Joseph does. We'll read on the bearskin rug as soon as you get back."

"Geehaw!" Papa called.

The Mi'kmaq camp became smaller, a cluster of wide tipi tents with smoke coming out the tops and beyond them, a line of canoes along the beach where the LeBlancs were already loading their things.

Elizabeth cried all the way home.

The Mi'kmaq camp became smaller, a cluster of wide tipi tents with smoke coming out the tops and beyond them, a line of canoes along the beach where the LeBlancs were already loading their things.

CHAPTER Nº 9

The LeBlancs were away for longer than a few days. A week passed. Every morning Elizabeth ran to the window to see if smoke rose above the little Acadian house. None did.

One day Papa rode to the fort to visit Lucien and invited Elizabeth to come along. Mama packed a basket of fresh food for Lucien to eat. After Papa explained to him where his family had gone, Lucien hung his head.

"We were so hopeful to buy land here and persuade other Acadians to come back. It was all a foolish dream," he said bitterly.

Lucien had been foolish to risk speaking to Sarah Worth. But Papa didn't criticize him and neither did Elizabeth.

"Much as I hate to see your family leave, I'm hopeful they'll see something they like around St. Mary's Bay."

"How can you say that?" Elizabeth cried.

"There's very little good land left here, and what there is will go first to English Protestants. That's how these things work. The LeBlancs would be the only French, Catholic family."

Lucien shook the bars of his small window. "Yes. We do know how these things happen. Papa's smart to look for land that isn't worth stealing. Somewhere Acadians can make a home without any English to hate them."

Elizabeth was about to deny this hotly, but Papa gave her a stern look.

Just before they left, she gave Lucien Sarah's message. He nodded, but that was all. Elizabeth didn't know what to make of it. Didn't Sarah matter any more? Whatever Lucien felt, she'd never know. Maybe he didn't know himself.

At home Elizabeth doted on her brother. She never tired of holding Joseph. She made up little songs for him, songs about his toes and fingers or about their move to Nova Scotia. She rocked him endlessly. When he cried, he sounded like a kitten mewling for milk and she ran to pick him up from his cradle.

Mama scolded her. "You can't pick him up every time he fusses."

"Why not?"

"Sometimes he needs time to settle himself. It's a good thing to learn. Even a baby has to wait. Count to a hundred before you go to him."

Elizabeth did so, but she'd never counted to a hundred so fast before.

Nine days after the LeBlancs had set out, Elizabeth had filled half a journal with notes about her baby brother. She looked up from the kitchen table where she sat writing. Was that the sound of voices outside?

She threw open the door and ran outside. The LeBlancs were trudging up the road through the early spring muck. Their clothes were splattered in mud but they waved and shouted when they saw her.

"Mathilde!" she screamed.

Mathilde ran to meet her, her black hair flying, her eyes bright. "Elizabeth!"

They hugged and danced when they met, mud flying everywhere.

"I missed you," they cried at the same time.

"Go change and bring me your dirty clothes," Mama called to the LeBlancs from the doorway. "I'll get a meal ready and a hot kettle. You can tell us your news at the table."

Before long they sat around the Brightmans' kitchen table eating bowls of thick soup. Between mouthfuls Joseph and his sons explained their journey and what they'd found. The land around St. Mary's Bay was mostly rocky but the fishing was excellent. There were already several Acadian families living there.

"They're going to help us build a new house."

"And a church next year and a priest will come."

"More Acadians are expected. We'll have our own town."

Elizabeth couldn't swallow. They were excited. She'd never seen them look so happy. She stole a glance at Mathilde. Mathilde was smiling like the rest of her family. Mathilde was going to move away!

Elizabeth dropped her spoon. Her stomach hurt. Joseph started to cry and she didn't bother to count to a hundred. She fled from the table to rock comfort into them both. It felt good to hold her baby brother. He stopped crying immediately and she felt powerful, as if she'd cast a good magic spell. He didn't like it when she sat so she paced in front of the fire. His face relaxed and his blue eyes stared eagerly into hers. Joseph would *never* leave her.

Mathilde came and stood beside her.

"Watch this," Elizabeth said and held out her finger for Joseph to grasp. Mathilde *oohed* when he did.

"Will he hold mine too? He's grown so much bigger already. Can I hold him? Please?" Mathilde begged eagerly.

Elizabeth shifted him carefully into Mathilde's arms.

"Do you really like it better in St. Mary's Bay than here?" she whispered, unable to hide her hurt.

Mathilde shook her head vehemently. "How can you ask that? Never better than here. But tomorrow, our papas will beg Captain Mercer to release Lucien. If we leave here, Caleb Worth should be satisfied. St. Mary's Bay should be far enough away. It took three days of steady paddling to get there." Mathilde's voice turned husky and her eyes grew shiny. "It was nice to speak French all the time. For the first time in a long time, I felt like I did when I was little. Before the deportation. It was a good feeling."

Elizabeth tried to imagine living on the outside of a community all the time and speaking a different language, but she couldn't. It was simply too wonderful to have Mathilde back, her family noisy and laughing, in their house. Something told her it wouldn't last long. She forced herself to smile at Mathilde. She was going to enjoy every last day and hour they had together.

Come evening all the chores were done and the LeBlancs gathered in the Brightmans' parlour. Mr. Porter dropped by with Joshua and Ginny and, to everyone's amazement, Sarah Worth and her mother.

Sarah stayed at the door, unusually quiet, and Elizabeth guessed she wanted to apologize. She whispered her suspicion in Mama's ear.

Mama took Sarah and her mother by the hand and said, "Follow me into the kitchen, my dears. We'll bring hot apple cider for everyone. Mireille, could you come too?"

Mathilde watched the women folk leave the parlour and nudged Elizabeth. "Something's up. Shouldn't we help too?"

Elizabeth whispered back. "Sarah's going to apologize."

"I don't want to miss that. How long should we wait?"

"Same as for baby Joseph. We have to count to a hundred."

They counted by twos to a hundred and then peeked around the kitchen doorway. Sarah must have given her apology already, for she was red-faced and teary. Madame LeBlanc was wiping away a few tears of her own.

Mathilde's mother faced Sarah's mother and said proudly, "Mr. Brightman, he talk wit' Captain Mercer tomorrow, so my son don' go to English prison. We take him an' move far away."

Rebecca Worth's face went pale, and she pressed her right hand against her chest. "I'm sorry it came to this."

"*Moi aussi.*" Madame LeBlanc motioned to Mathilde. "Time to read. You girls bring *les biscuits.*"

She lifted a platter with mugs and a pitcher of hot apple cider. Elizabeth and Mathilde moved into the kitchen to let her pass. Mama and Rebecca Worth followed her quietly.

The girls were alone now in the kitchen. Sarah looked up, first at Elizabeth and then at Mathilde, sadder than Elizabeth had ever thought possible.

"I liked your brother so much, Mathilde. All of you. And now I've driven you all away. What can I ever do to make it up to you?"

There was a long silence. They heard laughter coming from the parlour. The men didn't have a clue what had happened in the kitchen.

Mathilde said, "I don't know." She held one of the treasures from Pirate Island. She sat at the table and opened the book slowly. "Want to know something strange? Every time I read a story called *The Blue Bird*, I think of you and Lucien."

"Me too!" cried Elizabeth.

"What's it about?" asked Sarah.

"A princess and prince who love each other but are separated. They stay true to each other for years. If it's like that between you and Lucien," Mathilde rolled her eyes, "I suppose a separation won't matter."

Sarah's eyes filled with hope. "Do you really think so?"

Mathilde made a face. "I hope not. It's beyond me what you see in him. You've never watched him wring a chicken's neck. I think he *likes* it."

Just then Ginny peeked around the doorway. "Is this private?"

"Girls only," Elizabeth said. "Hurry up and sit down. Mathilde's going to tell us a French fairy tale. Written," she whispered dramatically, "by a woman."

Their eyes went round as Elizabeth lit a candle and Mathilde began the story. Once, Mama poked her head inside, saw that they were busy, and left with the biscuits. When Mathilde reached the end of the story, all four girls were quiet.

"*Merci*," Sarah said finally.

Mathilde laughed. "Your accent is still awful. You'd best take French lessons if you hope to impress Lucien in a few years."

Sarah grew serious. "If your father and Mr. Brightman are going to petition Captain Mercer to release Lucien tomorrow, Mama and I will talk to my father tonight. If you move away," she said sadly, "he'll be pleased. It's exactly what he wants."

"It doesn't seem fair," Elizabeth said hotly. "Something good should come of this." She said a quick prayer and then voiced her hope. "Could your mama ask for something precious in return?"

"What?" Sarah said dully. "What could possibly be as precious as a family leaving their home?"

"Freedom," Elizabeth said.

Sarah and Mathilde followed Elizabeth's gaze. All three girls stared at Ginny. Ginny lifted her chin. "If you talkin' about a dream of freedom, that be mine."

Sarah nodded. "I know you asked me before, Elizabeth, and I promised to try. But my mother didn't know if she could run the house without you and your mama, Ginny. But now that all this has happened and the LeBlancs are moving away, I'll talk to my mother again."

When the evening was over, Elizabeth said prayers for her family, for the LeBlancs, and for Joshua Porter and his father, and ended with one for Ginny and her mother.

Please God. Find a way to move Caleb Worth's heart tomorrow.

Papa and Joseph LeBlanc left for the fort early the next morning. Elizabeth begged to go with them, but Papa ordered her to stay home and help Mama.

She and Mathilde gave baby Joseph a bath in a basin by the fire. His skin was silky smooth, and in only a few weeks he'd turned almost chubby. They dressed him, swaddled him in a soft cotton blanket, and settled him to sleep in his cradle.

Mama had fallen asleep in her rocking chair. Spring sunshine poured in the windows and the kitchen was too warm.

Elizabeth grabbed Mathilde's hand and motioned to the door. They tiptoed outside.

Once outside they ran down the road to the dykes. The air was crisp and invigorating. The ground had mostly dried after a week of sunshine and the girls leapt over a few mucky puddles. They stood looking out at the bay. The waves sparkled. It was high tide and Pirate Island seemed a long way off.

Mathilde picked up a flat rock and made it skip across the water.

"How far away did you say St. Mary's Bay is?" Elizabeth asked.

"Three days in a canoe."

Elizabeth groaned. "How will you have time to visit this summer? Your papa will be too busy building a house and boat, plowing a first field."

Mathilde threw another rock and it skipped twice before disappearing. "Sometimes I hate Lucien! This is all his fault."

"You don't mean that!" Elizabeth said, horrified.

Mathilde turned to face her. Her black eyes were smouldering. "I don't want to go now. You're my best friend and this has been home again for us."

Elizabeth nodded sadly. "I had so many plans for us this summer. Will we ever get to go to Pirate Island together?"

Behind them on the road, they heard the sound of a wagon and oxen. Elizabeth turned to see Papa and Joseph LeBlanc. Beside them, Lucien sat, holding the reins in one hand, waving cheerfully at them with the other.

Mathilde began to run, Elizabeth right behind her.

"You're free!" Mathilde yelled.

Her brother stopped the wagon, handed the reins to his father, and jumped to the ground. He caught Mathilde, swinging her about before giving her a hug.

Elizabeth's heart warmed at the sight. Even if she was mad at him, Mathilde loved her brother.

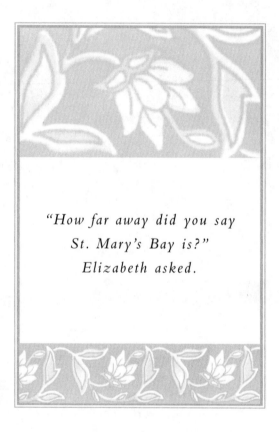

"How far away did you say
St. Mary's Bay is?"
Elizabeth asked.

"Was Caleb Worth there?" Mathilde asked her father.

"What did Captain Mercer say?" Elizabeth asked Papa.

"Whoa, girls. So many questions. Captain Mercer wished the LeBlancs well. And Caleb Worth was there. So was his wife. In fact, he apologized in his own way that the LeBlancs had to move away. I'm losing my farm help, and he feels responsible." Papa's voice turned gruff. "I don't expect him to understand that we're losing our friends. But we were only too happy to see Lucien released."

Joseph LeBlanc clapped Papa on his shoulder. "Mireille won' stop blessing you when she see her Lucien, safe and sound."

Papa's eyes narrowed. "There was an even stranger thing, however. Caleb Worth brought his two household slaves with him. Said he had to get Captain Mercer to sign some document. He was going to free Ginny's mother."

Elizabeth's knees buckled.

"Did you hear that, Mathilde?" she said.

Mathilde looked at her, transfixed.

"Ginny, too?" Elizabeth asked, not daring to hope.

"No. Just Ginny's mother. They'd saved up ten dollars over the years, enough to buy her mother's freedom. Ginny remains their household slave."

Elizabeth's eyes filled. Their plan had failed. Ginny wasn't free.

Papa's voice turned gruff. "I'm sorry you didn't see their faces. I've never seen a mother and daughter weep for joy as those two did when Captain Mercer gave Ginny's mother her document of freedom. She'll stay working at the Worth household, same as always, except for wages. The document states they can buy Ginny's freedom when she turns eighteen for another ten dollars. Something tells me that's just what they're fixing to do."

Elizabeth and Mathilde held hands and swung them. "Something good did happen. Ginny's mama is free! She's free!"

The other men looked down at their daughters, shaking their heads. Lucien climbed back into the wagon.

Joseph LeBlanc tipped his hat. "It look like another prayer answered. If these two girls stay together this summer, I wonder what miracle might happen next? What you think, Samuel?"

Elizabeth's papa winked at her. "We'd love to have Mathilde stay. It's up to Elizabeth. I'm not so sure she'll want to share her room or her brother with anyone—"

Elizabeth leapt up on the wagon and threw herself at Papa, crying, "Do you mean it? Can Mathilde stay? All summer! Of course I'll share my room with her."

Papa hugged her back. His face was rough and scratchy, but she didn't mind at all.

"You're the best papa in the world," she said. Then she hugged Mathilde's father. "You too!" She jumped off the wagon and smiled at Mathilde. "Do you want to stay? Please, Mathilde?"

Mathilde nodded, her eyes sparkling. "Until the new house is ready and they send for me. Maybe you can visit and our friends will paddle you back before winter."

"Slow down, girls. First we have to ask your mothers."

The wagon continued down the road, heading home.

Elizabeth had never known so much to be thankful for. Above them, the sky was deep blue, spotted with a few white clouds. Spring was in the air. Mathilde could stay! And Mama would surely agree to let Elizabeth visit the LeBlancs later.

It felt as if she had a new brother *and* a sister. Nova Scotia had grown ever so much bigger—or was it smaller?—in the last few minutes.

"Watch this, Mathilde. I've thought of a new game. Guess what I'm trying to be?"

Elizabeth lifted her skirt as wide as wings and ran down the dyke road. Mathilde would have no trouble guessing. They could stay together all summer. Now that Mathilde could read and write, they could stay in touch with letters when they were apart. Her prayers *had* been answered. Nova Scotia had become a home for them all.

Acknowledgements

THANKS TO MARTHA SCOTT AND THE LIBRARIANS
OF THE OSBORNE COLLECTION, WHO SHARE THEIR KNOWLEDGE
OF EARLY CHILDREN'S BOOKS SO GENEROUSLY.

Dear Reader,

*This has been the fourth and final book about
Elizabeth. We hope you've enjoyed meeting and
getting to know her as much as we have enjoyed
bringing her—and her wonderful story—to you.*

*Although Elizabeth's tale is told, there are still
eleven more terrific girls to read about, whose
exciting adventures take place in Canada's past—
girls just like you. So do keep on reading!*

*And please—don't forget to keep in touch! We love
receiving your incredible letters telling us about your
favourite stories and which girls you like best. And
thank you for telling us about the stories you would
like to read! There are so many remarkable stories
in Canadian history. It seems that wherever we
live, great stories live too, in our towns and cities, on
our rivers and mountains. We hope that Our
Canadian Girl captures the richness of that past.*

Sincerely,
Barbara Berson
Editor

Canada's

1608
Samuel de Champlain establishes the first fortified trading post at Quebec.

1759
The British defeat the French in the Battle of the Plains of Abraham.

1812
The United States declares war against Canada.

1845
The expedition of Sir John Franklin to the Arctic ends when the ship is frozen in the pack ice; the fate of its crew remains a mystery.

1869
Louis Riel leads his Metis followers in the Red River Rebellion.

1871
British Columbia joins Canada.

1755
The British expel the entire French population of Acadia (today's Maritime provinces), sending them into exile.

1776
The 13 Colonies revolt against Britain, and the Loyalists flee to Canada.

1837
Calling for responsible government, the Patriotes, following Louis-Joseph Papineau, rebel in Lower Canada; William Lyon Mackenzie leads the uprising in Upper Canada.

1867
New Brunswick, Nova Scotia, and the United Province of Canada come together in Confederation to form the Dominion of Canada.

1870
Manitoba joins Canada. The Northwest Territories become an official territory of Canada.

1762
Elizabeth

Timeline

1885
At Craigellachie, British Columbia, the last spike is driven to complete the building of the Canadian Pacific Railway.

1898
The Yukon Territory becomes an official territory of Canada.

1914
Britain declares war on Germany, and Canada, because of its ties to Britain, is at war too.

1918
As a result of the Wartime Elections Act, the women of Canada are given the right to vote in federal elections.

1945
World War II ends conclusively with the dropping of atomic bombs on Hiroshima and Nagasaki.

1873
Prince Edward Island joins Canada.

1896
Gold is discovered on Bonanza Creek, a tributary of the Klondike River.

1905
Alberta and Saskatchewan join Canada.

1917
In the Halifax harbour, two ships collide, causing an explosion that leaves more than 1,600 dead and 9,000 injured.

1939
Canada declares war on Germany seven days after war is declared by Britain and France.

1949
Newfoundland, under the leadership of Joey Smallwood, joins Canada.

1885
Marie-Claire

1897
Emily

1940
Ellen